Formula 1

D0806685

Contents

Written by Mary Colson

 Collins

The history, the teams and the drivers

Motor racing began in Europe in the 1920s and 1930s. Drivers raced around towns on normal streets. In 1947, Formula 1 was born.

This race took place in France in 1923.

"Formula" means rules that must be followed.
A Formula 1 race is called a grand prix,
which means "big prize".

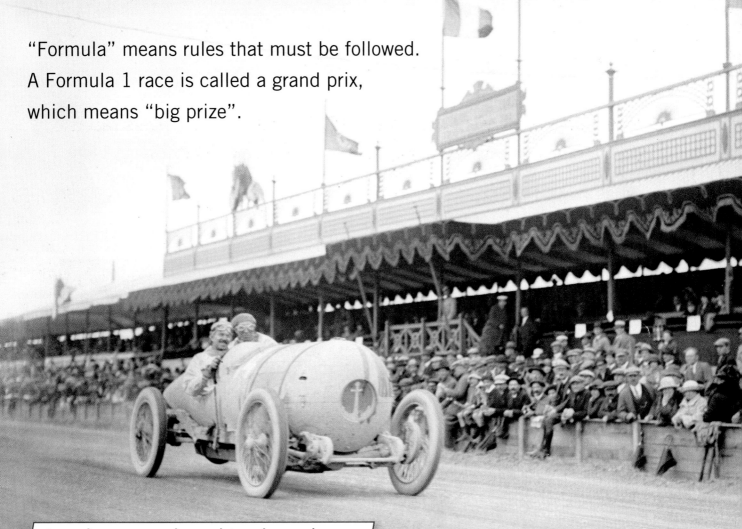

It took two people to drive the early
Formula 1 cars, like this one from 1922.

Track design

Each grand prix race is different. Some races are on special race tracks and some are on closed roads through cities. Modern race tracks are designed to help the cars go as fast as possible. Drivers and their teams study the tracks and work out their race plans.

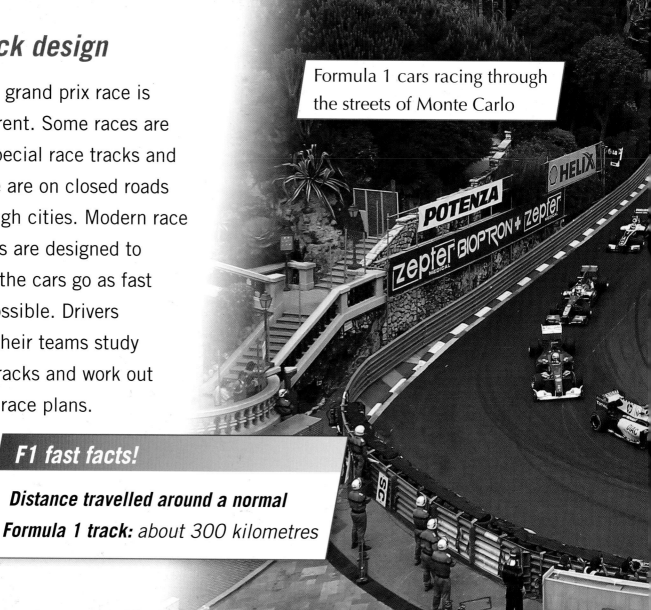

Formula 1 cars racing through the streets of Monte Carlo

F1 fast facts!

Distance travelled around a normal Formula 1 track: about 300 kilometres

The team

Famous Formula 1 teams include Ferrari, McLaren and Renault. Each team has two drivers and two cars. The drivers race against each other and against drivers from other teams.

Each driver has his own team of mechanics and engineers.

They work to make the car go as fast as possible.

The daredevil drivers

To be a Formula 1 driver, you need super-fast reactions and the strength, fitness and **stamina** of a top athlete. Driving a Formula 1 car is like being in charge of a rollercoaster. Your body is pushed and pulled in all directions.

Drivers have to wear a strong helmet to protect their head and neck when they're driving.

The race

Formula 1 races take place all over the world, from China to Brazil. There are 20 races in a season. The weather and track **conditions** change from place to place, so the teams need to adjust the cars for every race.

Special tyres are used to avoid skidding in wet weather.

On the grid

The day before
a grand prix,
the drivers compete
for their grid
position. This is
where they will start
from in the race.
If a driver is in pole
position it means
they start the race
at the front and
this can make
it easier to win
the race.

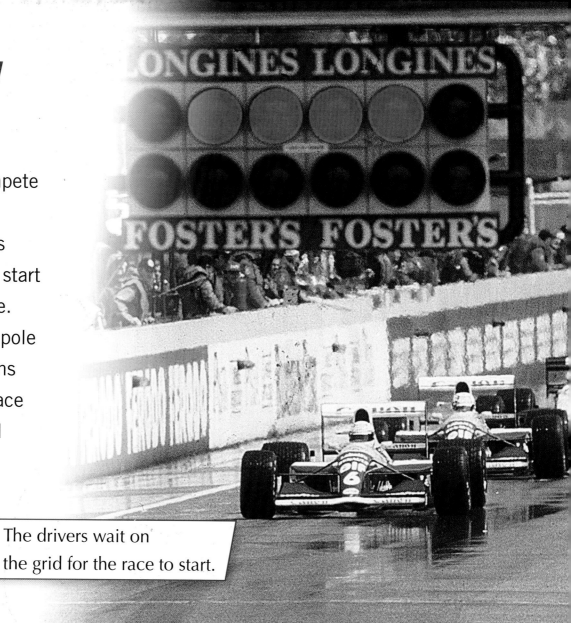

The drivers wait on
the grid for the race to start.

It's time to go racing!

When the starting lights
go out, the race begins.
The cars zoom forwards
and speed down the track,
overtaking if possible.
Drivers have to take
every corner and turn
as quickly as they
dare in order to win.

F1 fast facts!

Top speed: *about 320 kilometres per hour*

Fastest ever race speed: *369.1 kilometres per hour*

Fast and furious

Sometimes there are huge crashes. If this happens, the safety car goes out and all the cars have to slow down and are not allowed to overtake.

safety car

The pits and the prizes

During each race, the drivers must make a pit stop. The mechanics wait for the cars in the pit lane. More fuel and new tyres are added to the car.

a car reaching the pit lane

19

The big prize

The winner is the first
driver to race his car
across the line and see
the chequered flag waving.

Soon after, the teams
pack up the cars and kit.
Special planes take
the teams and the cars
to the next race.

The countdown to
the next grand prix
has already begun.

The top three drivers of each race celebrate on the **podium.**

A Formula 1 track

start grid

finishing line

danger – possible crash spot

safety car needed if there is a possible danger

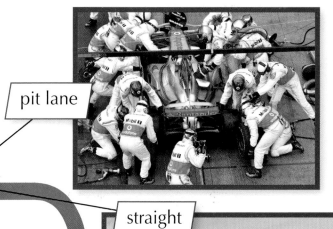

pit lane

straight

corner

Glossary

conditions   what something is like at a particular time

podium   platform

stamina   ability to keep going for a long time

Index

Ideas for reading

Written by Gillian Howell
Primary Literacy Consultant

Learning objectives: *(reading objectives correspond with Turquoise band; all other objectives correspond with Copper band)* read independently and with increasing fluency longer and less familiar texts; know how to tackle unfamiliar words that are not completely decodable; identify and make notes of the main points of section(s) of text

Curriculum links: Geography

Interest words: grand prix, special, cities, designed, mechanics, engineers, reactions, strength, athlete, chequered

Resources: pens, paper, drawing or modelling material

Word count: 476

Getting started

- Read the title and discuss the cover with the children. Ask them if they have heard of Formula 1 and what they know about it. Turn to the back cover and read the blurb together.

- Turn to the contents page and read the headings together. Ask the children if they think the text needs to be read in sequence or could be dipped into. Ask them to skim through the book quickly and then give a reason for their response.

- Pre-empt any problems with the pronunciation of foreign words. Turn to p3. Point out the phrase *grand prix* and give the children the pronunciation. Repeat this with *Renault* and *McLaren*.

Reading and responding

- Ask the children to read the book in pairs quietly. Listen in as they read and prompt as necessary. Remind them to use their knowledge of phonics and contextual clues to work out any words they are unsure of. Prompt them to look for words within words such as *rollercoaster* on p8.

- Pause occasionally to check the children understand what they are reading, e.g. on p10 ask them what the teams have to do when weather and track conditions change. On p12, ask them what *pole position* means.

- As they read, ask them to make notes of three key pieces of information that are new to them in the book to share with the group.